15 Very Easy Christmas Favorites

Arranged by Christopher DeSantis

Project Manager: Tony Esposito
Book Design: Ken Rehm
Recording by Blue Skies Productions
CD Performance by Christopher DeSantis

CW01390103

GOD REST YE MERRY, GENTLEMEN

TRADITIONAL
Arranged by CHRISTOPHER DE SANTIS

HARK! THE HERALD ANGELS SING

Lyrics by CHARLES WESLEY
Music by FELIX MENDELSSOHN
Arranged by CHRISTOPHER DE SANTIS

Adagio

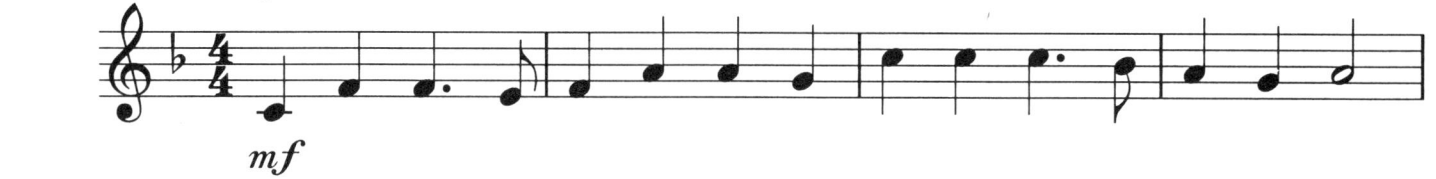

I HEARD THE BELLS ON CHRISTMAS DAY

Words by HENRY W. LONGFELLOW
Music by J. BAPTISTE CALKIN
Arranged by CHRISTOPHER DE SANTIS

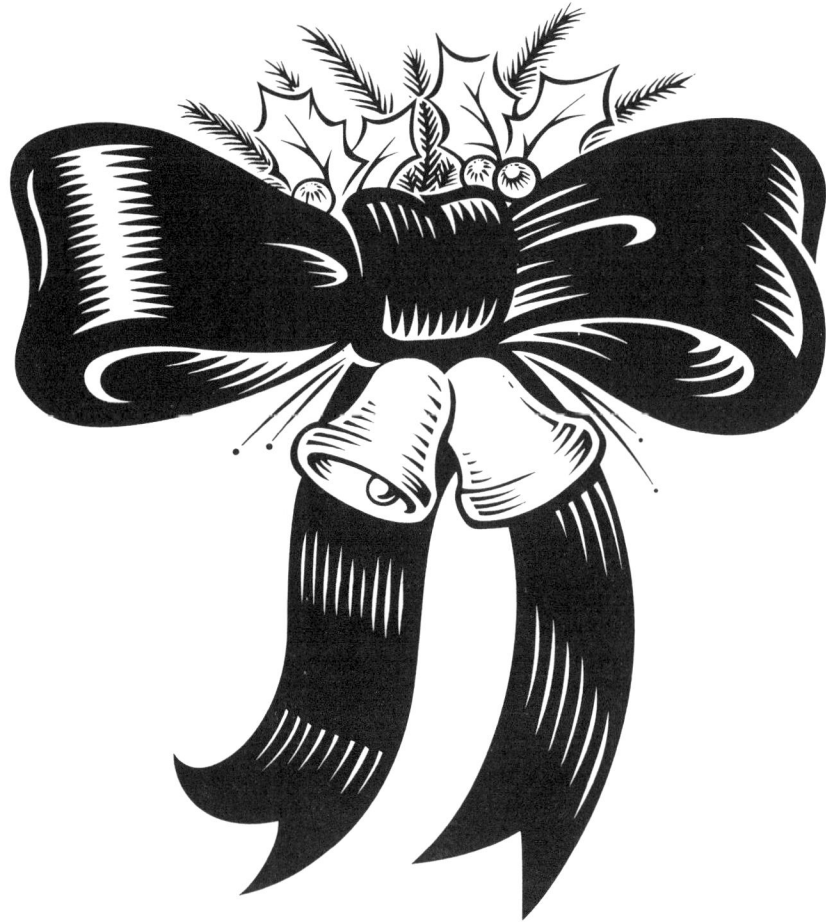

I SAW THREE SHIPS

TRADITIONAL ENGLISH
Arranged by CHRISTOPHER DE SANTIS

JINGLE BELLS

By JAMES PIERPONT
Arranged by CHRISTOPHER DE SANTIS

JOLLY OLD ST. NICHOLAS

TRADITIONAL
Arranged by CHRISTOPHER DE SANTIS

JOY TO THE WORLD

Words by ISAAC WATTS
Music by G.F. HANDEL
Arranged by CHRISTOPHER DE SANTIS

O CHRISTMAS TREE
(O Tannenbaum)

TRADITIONAL GERMAN CAROL
Arranged by CHRISTOPHER DE SANTIS

O LITTLE TOWN OF BETHLEHEM

Words by PHILLIPS BROOKS
Music by LEWIS H. REDNER
Arranged by CHRISTOPHER DE SANTIS

OVER THE RIVER AND THROUGH THE WOODS

EARLY AMERICAN SONG
Arranged by CHRISTOPHER DE SANTIS

SILENT NIGHT

Words by JOSEPH MOHR
Music by FRANZ GRUBER
Arranged by CHRISTOPHER DE SANTIS

Larghetto

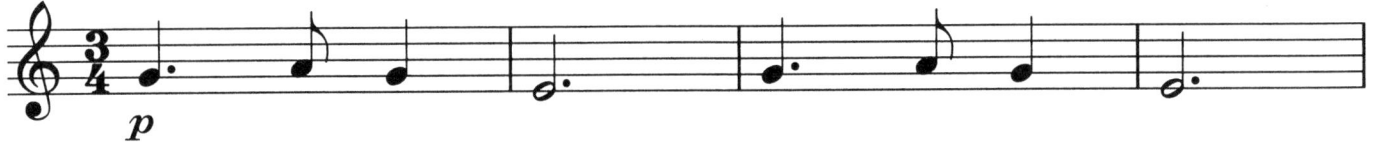

TOYLAND

Words by GLEN MacDONOUGH
Music by VICTOR HERBERT
Arranged by CHRISTOPHER DE SANTIS

UP ON THE HOUSETOP

B.R. HANBY
Arranged by CHRISTOPHER DE SANTIS

WHAT CHILD IS THIS?

OLD ENGLISH (GREENSLEEVES)
Arranged by CHRISTOPHER DE SANTIS

0141B

WHILE SHEPHERDS WATCHED THEIR FLOCKS

G.F. HANDEL
Arranged by CHRISTOPHER DE SANTIS